The Adventures of Scuba Jack

Little Duck was out for his morning stroll around the pond when he spied something shiny in the grass. He walked closer and noticed it was a beautiful pink egg. Next to the pink egg were some rather large footprints.

Who belongs to these footprints? he wondered. Where did this beautiful egg come from?

“That is a beautiful egg. Where did it come from?” asked Chick.

“I am not sure. I have been following these unusual footprints. Maybe if I find out who belongs to these footprints, I will find out where these eggs came from,” replied Duck.

“Can I join you?” asked Chick.

“Sure!” replied Little Duck.

Little Duck and Chick followed the footprints until they came upon a beautiful purple egg. Next to the egg were some carrots. The carrots looked like someone had taken bites out of them.

"What in the world?" asked Little Duck.

"Someone sure likes carrots!" said Chick.

"What a beautiful egg! Who does it belong to?" asked Lamb.

"We are not sure," said Little Duck.

"We have been following these unusual footprints. Would you like to join us?" asked Chick.

"Sure! I would love to!" said Lamb.

Little Duck, Chick, and Lamb followed the footprints until they came upon a beautiful golden egg. Next to the golden egg were some jellybeans.

"There sure are a lot of clues," said Little Duck.

"I love jellybeans!" said Chick.

"What a beautiful egg! Who does it belong to?" asked Fox.

"We are not sure," said Lamb.

"We have been following these unusual footprints," said Chick.

"Would you like to join us?" asked Lamb.

"Sure! I would love to!" said Fox.

Little Duck, Chick, Lamb, and Fox followed the footprints until they came upon a beautiful green egg. Next to the green egg was an Easter Basket.

"That's a beautiful basket," said Little Duck.

"Where did it come from?" asked Chick.

"I think these footprints are a clue," said Lamb.

"Who does this egg belong to?" asked Chipmunk.
"We don't know who the footprints belong to. We are going to follow them. Do you want to join us?" asked Fox

"Sure! I would love to!" said Chipmunk.

Little Duck, Chick, Lamb, Fox and Chipmunk followed the footsteps until they came upon a beautiful blue egg and glasses. "Who do these belong to?" asked Chipmunk. Little Bird also noticed the egg and glasses.

"Did someone drop this egg and glasses?" said Little Bird. "We don't know, but we are going to follow the footprints. Would you like to join us?" asked Fox. "Sure! I would love to!" said Little Bird.

Little Duck, Chick, Lamb, Fox, Chipmunk, and Little Bird followed the footprints.

"The footprints continue around those trees," said Little Duck.

"Let's follow them," said Lamb.

"This is an unusual forest," said Fox.

"The footsteps stop at a door," said Chick.

"I wonder who lives there," said Little Bird.

Little Duck, Chick, Lamb, Fox, Chipmunk, and Little Bird walked up to the door.
Little Duck reached out and knocked on the door.
“Maybe you should ring the bell,” suggested Chick.
“Good idea!” said Lamb.
“This is so exciting!” said Fox.
“I wonder who lives here,” said Chipmunk.

The door slowly opened and much to their surprise a bunny appeared. "Hello there! Can I help you?" asked the bunny.

Little Duck said, "We found these beautiful eggs and these chocolate bunnies, jellybeans, carrots, a basket, and glasses."

"Oh, my goodness! I must have dropped them! I have been so busy getting ready, I didn't even notice they were missing," said the bunny.

"What are you getting ready for?" asked Chick.

"Well, Easter of course! I am the Easter Bunny!" said the bunny.

"You're the Easter Bunny?" asked Lamb.

"Yes, I am! I sure could use help getting all these baskets ready! Won't you come in?" asked the Easter Bunny.

“Wow! This is amazing!” said Little Duck.
“Look at all those Easter Eggs,” said Chick.
“Those baskets are so beautiful!” said Lamb.
“How can we help?” asked Fox.
“Can you help me fill the baskets?” asked the Easter Bunny.
“Sure!” said Chipmunk.

The next day . . .
"I would like to make you honorary Easter Bunnies so you can help me deliver baskets," said the Easter Bunny.
"Sure! That would be fun!" said Little Duck.
Little Duck, Chick, Lamb, Fox, Chipmunk, and Little Bird put on bunny ears and a puffy, fluffy tail! They helped the Easter Bunny deliver all his baskets to all the children of the world.
So, if you spot a little duck, chick, lamb, fox, chipmunk, or little bird, just remember, they just might be the Easter Bunny's helpers!

www.ingramcontent.com/pod-product-compliance
Lightning Source LLC
Chambersburg PA
CBHW081137300726
48982CB00005B/980

* 9 7 8 1 0 8 7 9 8 9 0 5 1 *